To Leo and Toby — J.K.

For Gram and 阿婆. — K.S.

10% of all proceeds from the sale of this book will be donated to
Black and Pink, an organization in support of LGBTQ prisoners
that advocates for the abolition of prisons.
www.blackandpink.org.

Noodlephant

EXHIBIT B

Jacob Kramer

K-Fai Steele

ENCHANTED LION BOOKS
NEW YORK

Once there was an elephant who loved noodles. She loved noodles so much that all her friends called her Noodlephant. She loved to scoop noodles in huge slippery slurps and eat them by the trunkload.

She had neighbors of all sorts. Some had fur, some were smooth. Some could roll and some could fly. And some had deep pockets and were very, very bossy. Those were the kangaroos.

The kangaroos were always making new laws.

They made laws about who could swim at the beach
(only kangaroos)

who could enjoy the Butterfly Garden
(only kangaroos)

and who could make laws
(only kangaroos).

Noodlephant and her friends knew the laws weren't fair, but they didn't want to get thrown in the Zoo.

So instead of swimming at the beach, they cooled off in the sprinkler.

Instead of visiting the Butterfly Garden, they watched moths dance in lamplight.

Instead of making laws, they made food for each other.

Noodlephant in particular was famous for her pasta parties.
She loved to mix whole bags of semolina flour with dozens of eggs,
delighting her guests with noodles of all shapes and sizes.

For special occasions, she gathered wild mushrooms
to make her grandmother's secret sauce.

One day, while Noodlephant was shopping for a party, a kangaroo blew his whistle.

"You there, elephant! What are you doing with all those eggs and semolina flour?"

"Ummm," said Noodlephant, trying to stay calm, "I was thinking of a fresh batch of *fettuccine*? Maybe curly *cavatappi* would be nice. Or I could stretch a tangle of *tagliatelle*…"

"Oh no you won't!" snapped the kangaroo, pulling a law book from his pouch, "Elephants are no longer allowed to eat noodles. It says so right here: 'Noodles are for kangaroos. Elephants shall only eat sticks and branches.'"

"Maybe you don't know me," said Noodlephant, "But I'm *Noodle*phant. I'm all *about* noodles."

"You're an *ele*phant," said the kangaroo, "If we catch you eating noodles, we will lock you in the Zoo. Buy some acacia branches, and don't even *think* about noodles."

Walking home, Noodlephant couldn't help but think about noodles.
She thought about their shapes and colors, and all their slurpy sauces.

When her friends arrived, Noodlephant had nothing to offer them. She tried pouring tomato sauce on the acacia branches.

But they were not slippery. They were not slurpable. The thorns prickled and poked inside their bellies.

As Noodlephant gazed at her tender bellybutton, its shape reminded her of something…

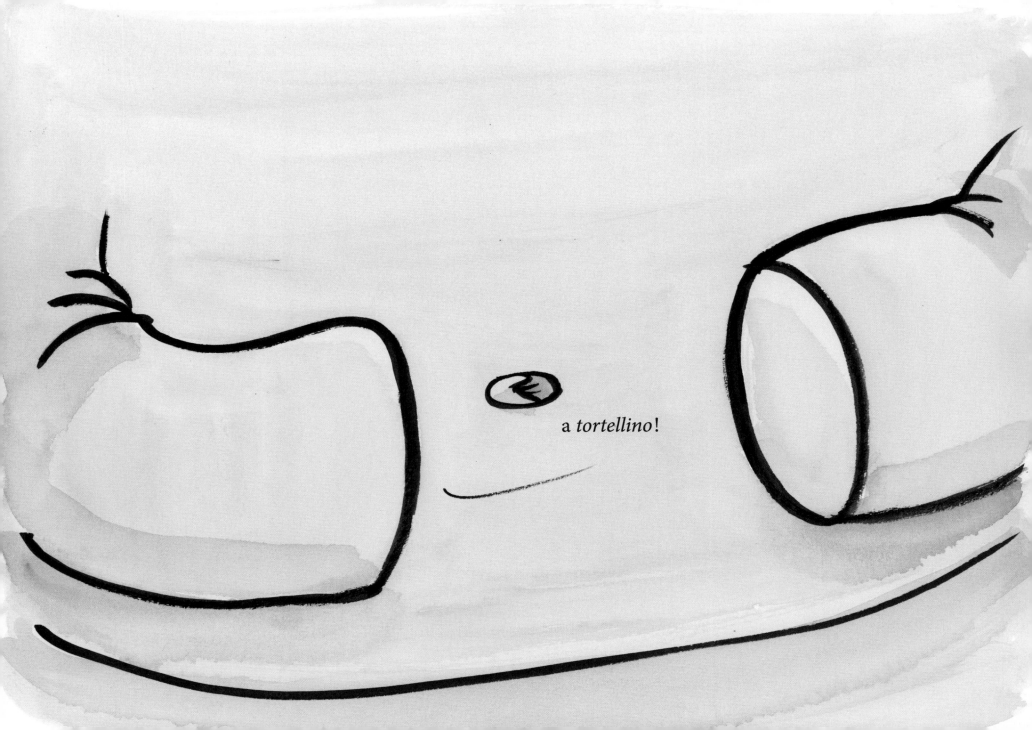

a *tortellino*!

All at once, she had an idea … A fantastic idea … A revolutionary idea for a completely new kind of machine.

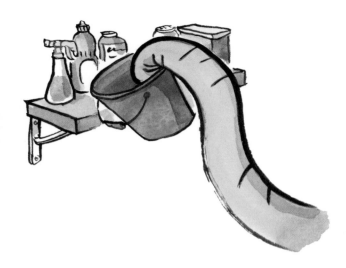

Together, Noodlephant and her friends tapped and tinkered, singing as they worked:

Those kangaroos are kanga-rude
Making rules about our food.
Telling us how we should think
What we can eat and what to drink.

When our new machine is done
We'll all eat pasta by the ton!
'Cause noodles are for me's and you's
Not just those bossy kangaroos!

They called the machine the Phantastic Noodler. It was very complicated, but also very simple. With a few turns of the crank, it could turn anything into noodles.

Noodlephant tossed in some pens. She turned the crank,
and out tumbled a pile of overcooked *penne*.

"Too soggy!"

She knocked a dent into the side,
and the next batch was perfectly *al dente*.

They looked around the house and found more stuff
to transform, cranking cans into *cannelloni*, pillows into *ravioli*,
and radiators into *radiatori*.

The noodles were slippery, slurpy, and scrumptious.
It was a grand pasta party, the best one yet.

That is, until …

The kangaroos tried Noodlephant in a kangaroo court.
They said she had broken the laws.

Noodlephant said the laws were already broken.

She declared:

The laws for elephants and shrews
Tortoises, fruit bats, and gnus
Should be the same as those we use
For all you wealthy kangaroos.

"Guilty!" said the judge.

As she was being led away, Noodlephant shouted,

Justice is for all of us,
Not just for the bossiest.
And though right now, it sounds absurd
One day, you'll want to eat your words!

Each day, a zookeeper brought Noodlephant a pile of thorny acacia branches,
and each day she refused to eat them. She was on strike.

Weeks passed, and Noodlephant got thinner and thinner.

When her friends visited,
they worried about her health.
They urged her to eat, but she
was resolute:

"The kangaroo laws aren't fair,
and everyone knows it. I'll starve
before I eat a single thorn."

Her friends called the kangaroos and wrote them letters. They protested outside the courthouse. Some kangaroos agreed the laws were wrong, but most didn't care.

And so, Noodlephant remained alone, stuck in the Zoo.
Her friends agreed they had to do something.

One lonesome day, Noodlephant received a letter.

DEAR Noodlephant,

WE KNOW YOU DON'T LIKE ACACIA BRANCHES, BUT WE WISH YOU WOULD TRY THEM TONIGHT. DEEP DOWN, YOU JUST MIGHT FIND THEY'RE PHANTASTIC!

LOVE, YOUR FRIENDS

That evening, Noodlephant accepted the zookeeper's pile of thorny branches.
She dug deep down with her trunk and found...

... the Phantastic Noodler!

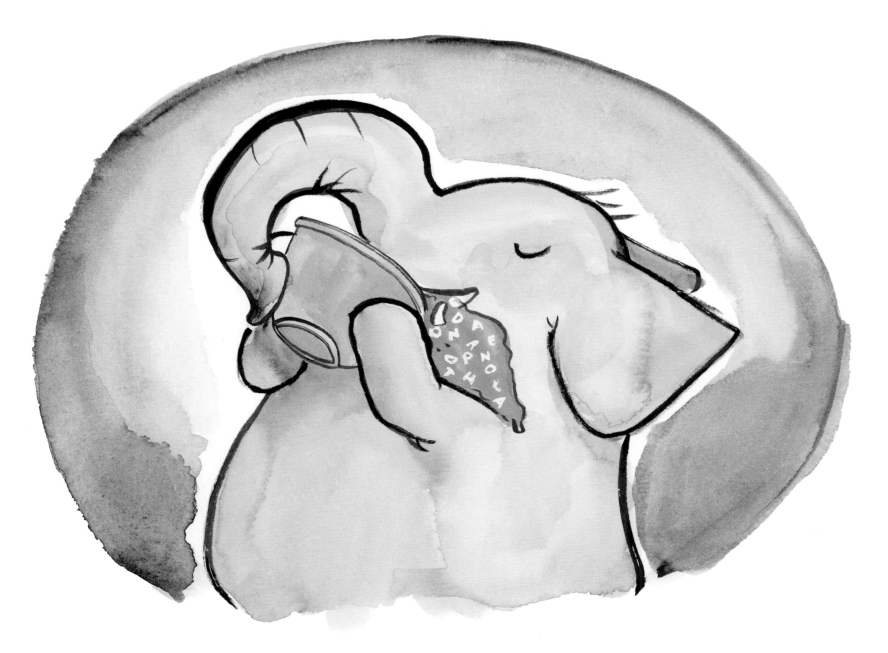

For an appetizer, she cranked the letter into a steaming bowl of alphabet soup.

Then Noodlephant clamped the machine to the bars of her cage.
Slowly and quietly, she turned the crank.

The iron bars collapsed into a pile of warm *udon*,
which she scooped up in slippery slurps.

She had never been so happy to see her friends.

They decided to throw a pasta party,
the like of which had never been seen.

Noodlephant's friends spread the word: everyone was welcome,
so long as they brought something to share.

As for Noodlephant, she knew the time had come to make something truly special.

She ventured deep into the forest to snuffle out wild mushrooms for her grandmother's secret sauce.

As the sun rose over the courthouse square,
the animals began to cook.

Smells wafted over the town. Sizzling onions mixed with simmering tomatoes; the tang of raw garlic blended with fresh basil and parmesan cheese.

Soon the guests began to arrive. Each animal brought something different to crank through the Phantastic Noodler.

Together, they turned corkscrews into *cavatappi*

flowers into *fiore*

and wheels into *rotelle*.

That is until …

"What do you all think you're doing here?"

"Welcome to our potluck," said Noodlephant, "Our guests have all brought something to share. Do you have anything to offer?"

The kangaroo brandished his law book, and began,
"The law is the law. It says right here: 'Noodles are for kanga–

"What a thoughtful contribution!" said Noodlephant.
With a flick of her trunk, she whisked the law book from the
kangaroo's paw, and cranked it through the machine.

Out came a piping hot slice of *lasagna*, covered in bubbling cheese!
She topped it off with mushroom sauce and gave it to the kangaroo.

It was the most delicious thing
he had ever tasted.

The other kangaroos lined up to crank their laws through the Phantastic Noodler, turning out tray after tray of mushroom *lasagna*.

The town celebrated long into the night, singing together:

When the laws are so unjust
Misbehavior is a must!
Together we will make new rules
To share along with fresh noodles.

'Cause noodles are for me's and you's!
We won't be locked up in the zoos
We'll slurp them down on avenues
At the beach and in canoes!

Yes, noodles are for me's and you's—
We'll even share with kangaroos .

Jacob would like to thank his nephew Leo for telling him about the elephant
who loved noodles, and his brother Matthew for bringing the first draft to life.

K-Fai would like to thank Marc Drumwright, for being the cleanup crew on *Noodlephant*.

www.enchantedlion.com

First edition published in 2019 by Enchanted Lion Books,
67 West Street, 317A, Brooklyn, New York 11222
Text © 2019 Jacob Kramer
Illustrations © 2019 K-Fai Steele
Art Direction: Claudia Bedrick
Layout and production: Marc Drumwright
A CIP record is on file with the Library of Congress
RR Donnelley Asia Printing Solutions Limited
ISBN: 978-1-59270-266-4
1 3 5 7 9 8 6 4 2